D0624270

To four bighearted animal lovers—
Koen MacKay, Paris Michelle Lipka, Enzo Jensen, and Aimee H.—
who make the world a brighter place
—L.A.

To my playful pup, Pippi,
whose personality is as big as her namesake's
—S.K.

 Published in the United States by Random House Children's Books,
a division of Penguin Random House LLC, New York.

Random House and the colophon are registered trademarks of Penguin Random House LLC.

Visit us on the Web! rhcbooks.com

Educators and librarians, for a variety of teaching tools,
visit us at RHTeachersLibrarians.com

Library of Congress Cataloging-in-Publication Data is available upon request.
ISBN 978-1-5247-6559-0 (trade) — ISBN 978-1-5247-6560-6 (lib. bdg.) —
ISBN 978-1-5247-6561-3 (ebook)

Book design by Nicole de las Heras

MANUFACTURED IN CHINA
10 9 8 7 6 5 4 3 2 1
First Edition

Random House Children's Books supports
the First Amendment and celebrates the right to read.

words by
Linda Ashman

pictures by
Suzanne Kaufman

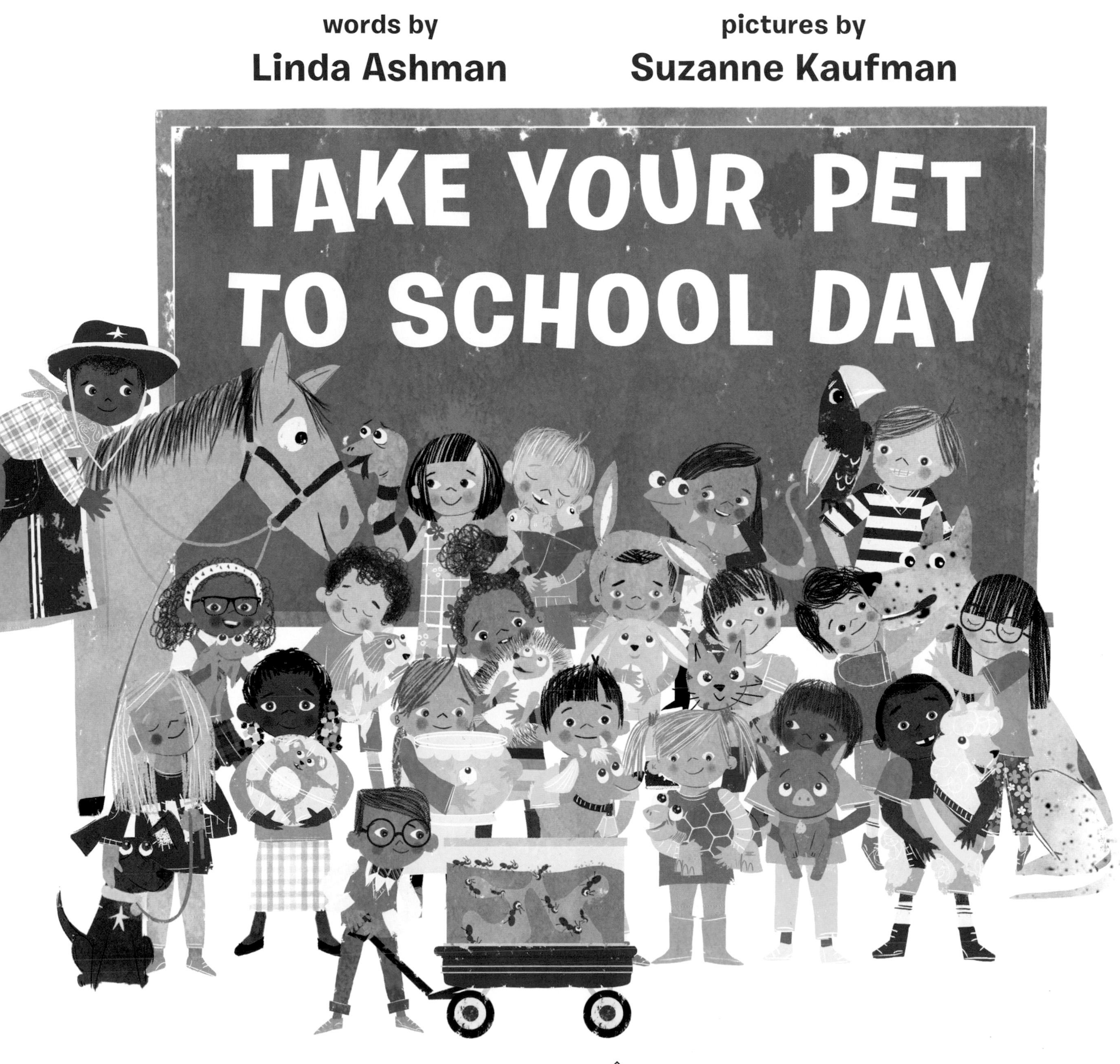

Random House New York

MAPLE VIEW SCHOOL

123 School Road • (123) 456-7890

Dear Students:

At Maple View, we have a rule:

You cannot bring your pets to school.

But—for just one special day—

we've decided it's okay

to bring your bunny, bird or dog,

your lizard, turtle, fish or frog.

So, this Friday—don't forget!—

we'll see you and your favorite pet.

Maple View School

It's Friday here at Maple View.
The students file in two by two,
with books and bags and pets in tow—
above, ahead, beside, below.

They start the day off with a song.

The pets attempt to sing along:

They howl with gusto, bleat with glee.

They shriek.
They squeak.
They're WAY off-key.

"Enough!" says Mr. Paul. "It's clear—
these animals should not be here.
Now, why would someone change this rule?
Pets do NOT belong in school!"

It’s story time. The pets pile in.
Ms. Libby, the librarian,
begins to read but can’t be heard
above the din of beast and bird.

They interrupt with barks and quacks.
They hide in nooks; they climb the stacks.

BARK

QUACK

QUACK

Ms. Libby sighs. "It's very clear—
these animals should not be here.
Now, why would someone change this rule?
Pets do NOT belong in school!"

She shoos them out, and off they go
to Mr. George's studio.

He tells the class, "We'll paint today—
the Art Show is a week away!"

The pets aren't neat.
They do not share.
Paint is spattered everywhere!

Says Mr. George, “It’s very clear—
these animals should not be here.
Now, why would someone change this rule?
Pets do NOT belong in school!”

Time for snack.
The pets won't sit.
They slurp and burp and drool and spit.
Rudely chomping, loudly chewing,
smacking, grunting, gobbling, spewing.

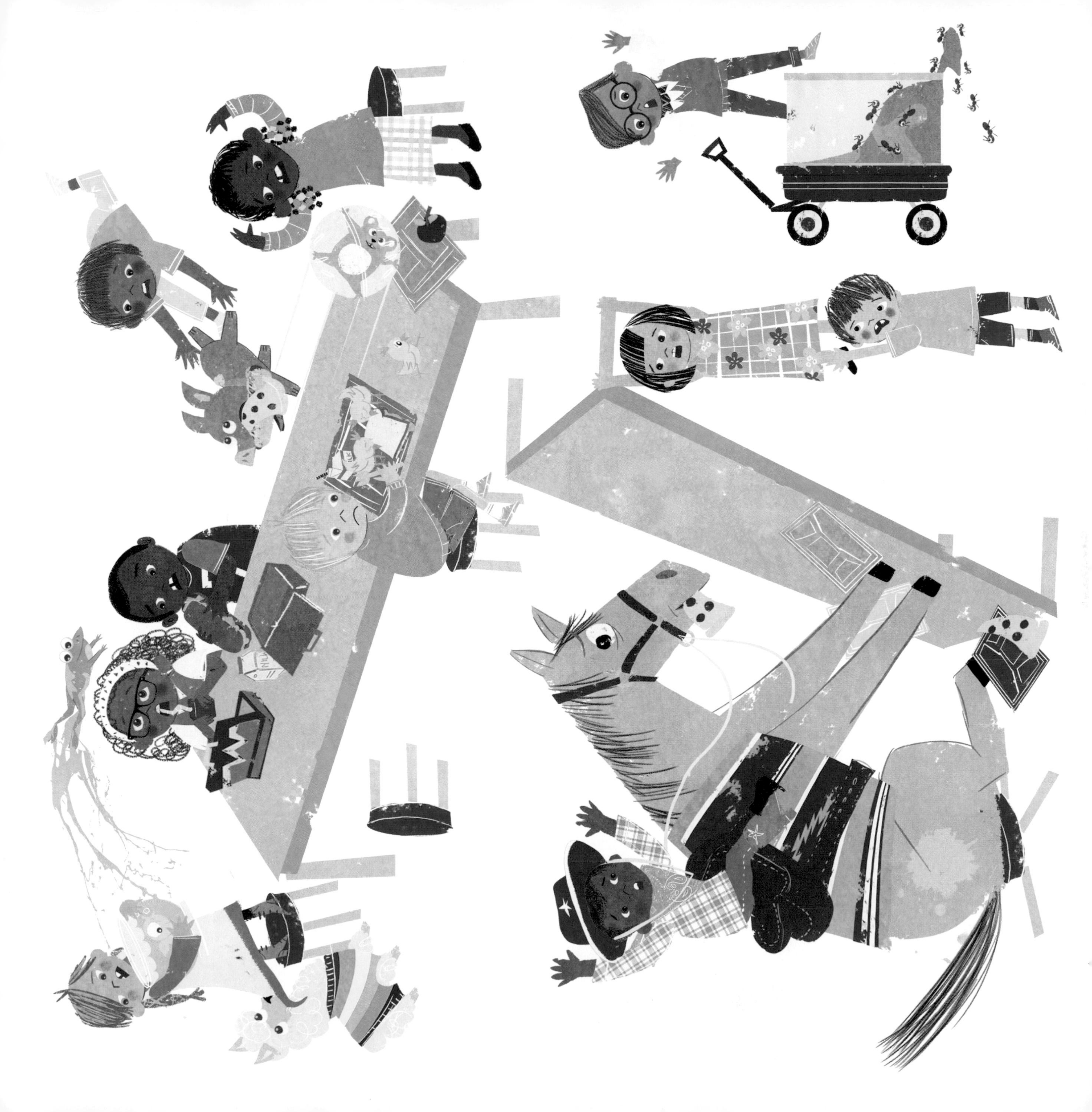

The principal is in a huff.
Ms. Ellen hollers, "That's enough!
This is NOT the way we eat.
Please settle down and take a seat."

She looks around. "It's very clear—
these animals should not be here.
Now, WHY would someone change this rule?
Who said these pets could come to school?"

The teachers shrug.

"Don't know."

"Not me."

"They don't belong here—we agree!"

Then Lucy whispers in her ear:
"*You* said we could.
Just look—right here."

Ms. Ellen says, “For goodness’ sake!
This isn’t mine! There’s some mistake.
Who wrote this note?
Speak up.
Right now.”

All is quiet.

Then . . .

“Meeoowww.”

We do not like your "No Pets" rule.

We miss our kids when they're at school.

We thought that it would be okay

to come to school – it's just one day.

♡ Pets

They wait in silence.

Still.

Polite.

She hems.

She haws.

She says . . .

“All right.
But ONLY if you clean this mess—
AND behave your very best.”

The pets agree.
They scrub with care.
They go to class,
take turns and share.
They follow rules and listen well.
They help with math and show-and-tell.

QUACK
QUACK

The school bell rings—it's time to go.
The kids depart with pets in tow.
Ms. Ellen breathes a weary sigh.
"Good work!" she says.
"Good job!
Goodbye!"

Dear Students:

At Maple View, we've had a rule:
You cannot bring your pets to school.
But your friends have been so good,
we've decided that you should!
So pack your hedgehogs, hounds and mice,
your cats and goats and snakes (if nice).
We love your pets, so it's okay
to bring them each and EVERY day!

Maple View School

OF COURSE
I'M AWESOME!
I'M A
PRINCIPAL!
PRINCIPAL
PRINCIPAL
PARKING
ONLY
VIOLATORS WILL
BE GIVEN
DETENTION!